The Night
The Three Pigs'
Christmas

Written by Larry Carney

PC Multimedia Entertainment
TREASURES, INC.

Published by

 PC Multimedia Entertainment TREASURES, INC.

2765 Metamora Road, Oxford, Michigan 48371 USA

The Night Before the Three Pigs' Christmas
Written by Larry Carney
Story Narration Performed by Nigel Lambert
Songs Written by Larry Carney
Songs Produced and Performed by Deron "D. B." Harris
Vocal Performances by Melissa Cusick and Deron "D. B." Harris
Illustrated by Brijbasi Art Press Ltd.

ISBN 1-60072-113-3

First Published 2008

'Twas the night before Christmas and snugly in bed,
The three pigs dreamed of the morning ahead,
When they'd throw back the covers and run to the den,
To see what Santa Claus had brought for them.

Would he bring them some toys? Oh, they so hoped he would.
They tried very hard all year long to be good.
Maybe shovels and rakes for their small garden plot,
And a shiny new trough for their dinnertime slop.

Such wonderful wonderings, such grand speculations,
Filled their sweet dreams with anticipation.
So, peacefully, pleasantly they dozed away
Knowing when they awoke it would be Christmas Day.

TURN PAGE

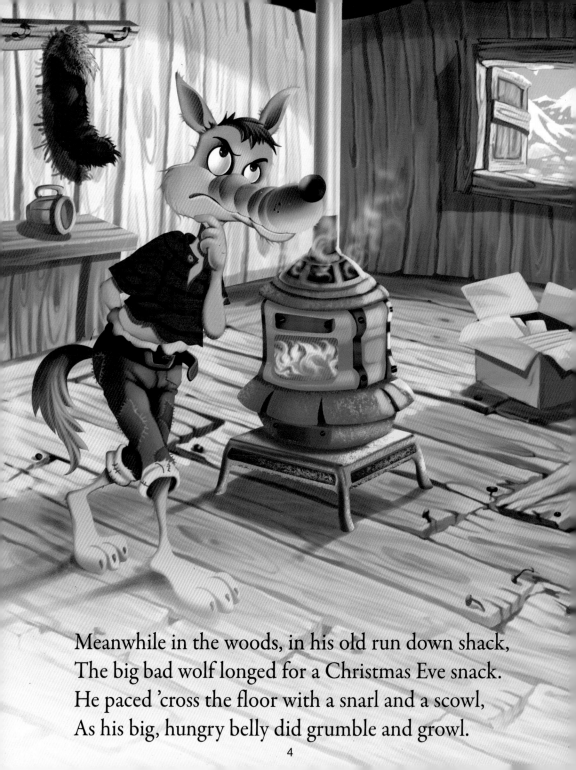

Meanwhile in the woods, in his old run down shack,
The big bad wolf longed for a Christmas Eve snack.
He paced 'cross the floor with a snarl and a scowl,
As his big, hungry belly did grumble and growl.

"What I wouldn't give for a dinner of pork!"
He muttered aloud as he walked back and forth.
"A nice pig would be fitting for my roasting pan,
After all, 'tis the season for a fine Christmas ham!"

"Now, there are those three pigs that I'd so love to catch.
But as I learned before, they are more than my match.
And not even my trusty, tried-and-true huff and puff
Has been able to get them – it's just not good enough."

"For though I blew down their houses of hay and of sticks,
I just can't blow over a house made of bricks.
And the chimney, oh no, that idea also failed,
And I only succeeded in burning my tail."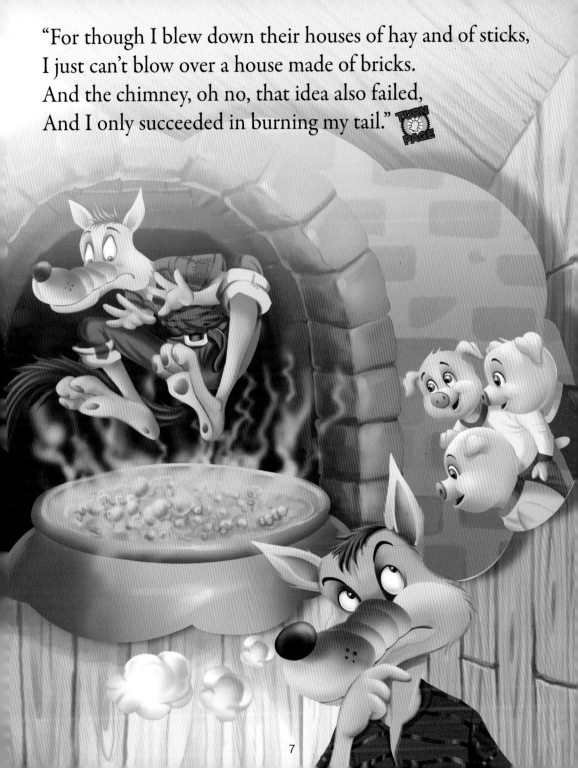

"No, I need to be clever if I want Christmas dinner.
I'll need an idea – one that's clearly a winner."
And he thought, and he paced 'til at last in his eyes
There came a sly look, "Of course! I'll use a disguise!"

"Tonight's Christmas Eve and St. Nick's expected.
That's how I'll get in their house undetected."
Then the wolf dressed in red from his head to his paws
And sneered, "Little pigs, prepare to meet Santa *Claws*!"

TURN PAGE

Well, the three little pigs were still dozing in bed
When a sudden noise woke them, they sat up and said,
"Did you hear that?" "Oh, yes!" "Yes, I heard it too!
Santa's arrived! He's up there on the roof!"

The three pigs jumped out of their beds with a bound.
"Oh, let's go to the chimney and watch him come down!"
So into the den the three of them ran,
Excited to greet the jolly old man.

When he came down the chimney, the pigs smiled with awe,
Unaware that it wasn't Santa at all.
In their joy they didn't notice that he was too thin
Or how the white whiskers were glued on his chin.

The disguised big bad wolf smiled down at the pigs,
As he tugged at his coat and adjusted his wig.
"Ho, ho, hoooooooooo!" said the wolf, as he tried to act jolly.
"And a fine season's eatin—er greetings to you pigs, by golly!"

TURN PAGE

13

"Merry Christmas, Santa!" the pigs cried with delight,
Still without any clue that things were not right.
"We left out some cookies we'd baked just for you!"
"A snack?" the wolf smiled. "Don't mind if I do!"

With that the wolf opened the sack that he'd brought,
And then one, two, three, those poor piggies were caught.
As he shouldered the sack, he heard the pigs shout,
"What's going on!? Santa Claus, let us out!"

TURN PAGE

"Oh, I'm afraid, piggies, that Santa's not here."
The big bad wolf said with an arrogant sneer.
"Oh no!" cried the pigs. "What a terrible fix!
We've fallen for one of the wolf's dirty tricks!"

The big bad wolf chuckled, "Now, don't get excited!
Christmas dinner's at my house, and you're all invited!"
And with that, he turned 'round to the chimney and saw,
Standing behind him, the real Santa Claus.

TURN PAGE

Santa Claus said, "Why wolf, I don't suppose
You'd like to tell me why you're dressed in those clothes?
And shouldn't you be back at home in your shack?"
Then Santa leaned close, "And what's that in your sack?"

"Why... er... hello there Santa! What a surprise!
Is it Christmas already? My how the time flies!
And as for this sack? Oh, it's full of... uh... wolf gear."
Just then the pigs cried, "Help! It's crowded in here!"

TURN PAGE

"Now you let those pigs go!" Santa Claus said.
The wolf set them free and then hung his head.
"Santa," he said, "I don't mean to be vicious.
"It's just that these three pigs all look so delicious."

Santa said, "Go back home, and I won't tell you twice,
And don't you return 'til you've learned to be nice!"
After the wolf had run off in the night,
Santa asked with a smile, "Are you piggies alright?"

"Oh yes, Santa Claus, we're just a bit shaken,
But thank you so much for saving our bacon!"
Santa Claus chuckled and tucked them in bed,
Then filled up their stockings and returned to his sled.

Then back in his sleigh, Santa happily called,
"Dash away reindeer, dash away one and all!
For tonight we shall visit many fine neighborhoods
Of people and piggies and wolves... that are good!"

Christmas is coming, that fine time of year,
When hearts of all ages are brimming with cheer,
So ring in the season with smiles big and bright,
And four Christmas tales to enchant and delight.

Stories Come Alive!

Original fairy tale books told in whimsical verse plus a CD jam-packed with fun-filled adventures!

Learn-to-Read Animation

Music Video

Coloring Pages

Audio Fun:
• Rhyming, chiming read-along
• Terrific toe-tapping tunes

PC Fun:
• Learn-to-read with highlighted text and story animation
• Bouncy music video
• Awesome coloring pages
• Printable storybook, lyrics, and coloring pages

CD-ROM works with Windows Vista/XP/ME/98

Collect Them All!

www.storiescomealive.com

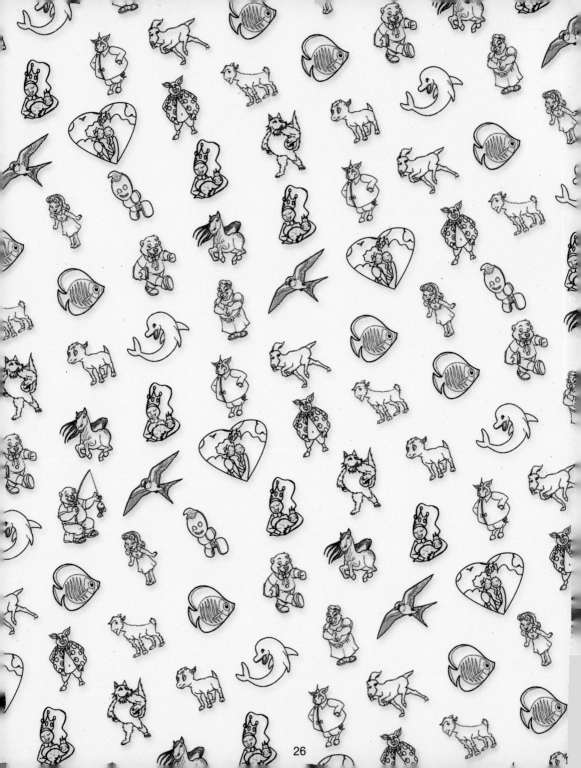